TIME TO GROW UP
AND
HANDLE YOUR SHIT!

A Guidebook for Young Adults

Bridget Higgins

Table of Contents

The intention of this little book is to inform you of one **OR** all of the following:

- The people who have raised you are exhausted.
- You are 18 years old (maybe older) and are now considered an additional household bill.
- You are loved, but this is your hint to leave the nest.
- It is time to handle your shit because all of us have our own shit to handle.

OLD FARTS
&
SUPERHEROES!

So...which old fart in your world decided to be a smart-ass and give you this book? Your parents? Grandparents? Uncle or Aunt?

Now that you have it, what will you do with this silly little book?
Will you throw it away?
Will you save it as a keepsake?
Maybe you will give it to a friend on their birthday because you are also a smart-ass.

Maybe, if you glance through this book, you will discover some useful information, which may assist you in handling your adult shit.

Book's terms—

The term, '*old farts,* 'refers to a special group of
people who consists of everyone older than you, who
you view as old. The term *'superheroes,* 'refers to
'you' and all of your people who are younger than 'us'
old farts.

Superheroes possess powers within their
youthfulness, which consists of high levels of energy
and above average intelligence (so you believe).

Many superheroes think they know everything they
need to know when becoming an adult, and do not
need advice from an old fart. Maybe the superheroes
feel that taking advice from an old fart is not really
going to assist them in any way because more often
than not, the old farts surrounding them need the
superheroes to assist with technological devices &
software applications. 'Us' old farts understand this
way of thinking because we actually had similar
thoughts at your age.

Try to find the time to read this little book...like
when you are sitting on the toilet. There may be
something written within the contents of this book
that just might help you one day!

Street Smarts
for
Old Farts!

To be 'street-smart,' you must carry an awareness about you every day!

The following list of driver safety reminders should be in the forefront of your thoughts when you are out-and-about on the planet; these are things not always discussed in driver's education courses, and 'us' old farts may forget to tell you because we are old.

Driving Safety Reminders

- Get a roadside assistance plan as soon as you begin driving— in the end it will save you money and you will have peace-of-mind that someone will come help you wherever you are on the planet with your car. Roadside assistance plans are affordable— the annual cost for most plans usually equals to the cost of one towing service.
- Always take your cell phone and a car phone charger in your vehicle...everyone knows this shit, but I just have to state it for the book.
- The first two things to do when you get into your car is to buckle-up (remind your passengers) and lock the doors.

- Keeping jumper cables in your car is smart but roadside assistance is the way to go.
- Always have a service center check your car's tires, fluids, and wiper blades—tire blowouts at high speeds can take you and others around you off the planet!
- Do not text & drive (search the stats on the deaths caused by texting and driving).
- Never drink and drive— your family or friends will pick you up (even if you are a pain-in-the-ass) or you can always taxi home.
- Do not turn your head towards your passenger(s) when driving and talking...it only takes a second to crash.
- Do not reach down to pick-up anything while you are driving.
- If you spill a drink while driving, clean it later or drive home to clean up & change your clothes if necessary...just don't freak-out while driving!
- Do not place pets on your lap while driving because animal behaviors are unpredictable.
- Do not speed or swerve around cars because you are running late or because you are frustrated with the old fart driving in front of you...it could be an old fart relative or a friend's old fart relative, so have some respect for the old farts!

- Do not open your car window to anyone on the streets…there's too many freaks! In addition, freaks can look normal & nice— Google 'Ted Bundy' if you have not heard about that clean-cut guy. In other words, 'The Boogie-Man' is not always the person that looks scary!
- Do not ever sleep in your car— you never know who may be lurking around rest stops and parking lots. Always budget for a hotel during road trips to get your rest and to stay safe.
- When traveling by car, always carry a small cooler filled with water bottles and snacks, in case you are left waiting a long time for roadside assistance.
- You should not eat and drive—one never knows when a sneeze or a cough will fly out of your face and cause you to choke while driving (it has happened).
- Do not pull over on the interstate, highways, or bridges (really anywhere) to assist someone with car troubles. There have been cases where people were set-up and attacked— cases where people believed they were helping a stranded woman on

the highway, when in fact, the so-called stranded woman's boyfriend was hiding in the bushes and attacked the Good Samaritan (now a victim). The only good deed necessary to assist others on the road is to call the highway patrol and report the person's location.

- Do not offer to give strangers a ride, no matter how nice they appear. Tell them to call a taxi or the police for assistance (better to just ignore them and haul-ass away before they car-jack you or worse).

- Do not drive or ride with anyone, which you suspect does drugs...only bad shit comes from drugs!

- If you live in a state where it snows or are driving to a state, which may experience snow, make sure you have the appropriate snow tires on your vehicle or your car will become a sled. Also, make sure you have blankets and snacks in the car in case the car breaks down.

- Never leave an animal or a child in a vehicle— (again, I just have to state this...sadly, people still do this shit).

- Be cautious of animals crossing the roads & highways. This topic is difficult to suggest possible precautions other than to drive with caution and focus, especially in areas without streetlights and on roads where you see posted 'Wildlife Crossing' signs.
  FYI: Hitting a large animal at high speeds can be the equivalent of hitting another vehicle head-on.
- Lastly, set reminders to pay your car insurance premium each month. Driving without car insurance is a liability you cannot afford...one accident without insurance and you injure a passenger in your car, in another car, or a pedestrian— may result in a garnishment of your wages for many years to come to cover their injuries.

Driving is a privilege and the law can take away those privileges— indefinitely! Driving laws protect everyone on the road...you, your family, your friends, children, strangers, and all of 'us' old farts!
Keep in mind— everyone on the road is someone's family member—you would not want someone to harass or drive dangerously around your old fart parents & grandparents!

SHIT HAPPENS!

Most of us feel bad when we hear about others dealing with bad shit. Many superheroes cannot imagine anything bad happening to them because they are invincible! If you are one of those superheroes, maybe it is time to revise your logic.
Many times when shit happens, it is beyond our control, even when we put forth our best efforts to be responsible adults.

Responsible adults keep an awareness about them and share our knowledge with our children and young adults, who cannot stand hearing 'Us" old farts lecture. More often than not, their knowledge is heightened from witnessing bad situations that has happened to someone they know or maybe has happened to them way-back in their superhero days.

Responsible adults know that shit happens, therefore, they purchase various types of insurance policies. Having certain insurances in place will ease the financial burden caused from a shitty accident or situation, which may result in lawsuits.

The following list is for those who do not have a basic understanding of the different types of insurance policies. Contact a local insurance agent for further insurance information.

- **<u>Auto Insurance</u>**- Always read your auto policy and review it with your insurance agent...you never want to say, "I thought I had..."

  Below is an example of what you should know about your auto policy:
  - ✓ The amount of liability coverage for passengers in your vehicle, and drivers/passengers of any other vehicle(s) involved.
  - ✓ The amount of collision coverage to repair or replace your vehicle— if necessary.
  - ✓ Medical benefits.
  - ✓ Daily car rental benefits.
  - ✓ Ask if roadside assistance comes with the policy or if it is available to add-on.
  - ✓ Have an agent explain your deductible to you if you are uncertain how deductibles work.

✓ If you tow a trailer or a recreational vehicle from your car/truck, ask your agent about the coverage & liability— for instance, what happens if your boat trailer disconnects from your car and hits another vehicle(s)?

- <u>Life Insurance</u>- This is the one type of insurance policy many people like to avoid.

  ✓ Most life insurance companies require you to have a medical exam.
  ✓ The younger you are when you get life insurance, the better the rate so you should consider purchasing a life policy while you are a youthful superhero.
  ✓ Ask your insurance agent to explain the various life policies available and always comparison shop.

✓ If you already have kids and you do not have life insurance, seriously consider using your superpowers to fly-out and get some life insurance! Your partner/spouse and children will have enough emotional issues in the event you suddenly exit the planet and they do not need financial issues on top of a tragedy—like losing the family home.

- <u>Health & Dental Insurance-</u> Many people will obtain health & dental insurance through their employer. You would be wise to become familiar with your healthcare policy in order to fully understand how your future medical claims will be paid, and how your deductible applies to those claims over a calendar year. If you do not have health/dental insurance through your employer, there are many resources available online... you can search for local health insurance agents/brokers to assist you (always check insurance brokers & healthcare companies with the 'BBB'-Better Business Bureau).

- <u>Home Owners Insurance-</u> This insurance is for possible future damages to your home and may provide additional financial protection in the event someone bust their ass on your property.

- <u>Renter's Insurance-</u> Many rental agreements require tenants to have 'renter's insurance' to cover the replacement cost of their personal belongings in the event the rental unit/home were damaged/destroyed.

- <u>Personal Liability Insurance-</u> This type of insurance assists with additional financial protection against personal liability cases (potential lawsuits) and usually purchased by those with many assets. Consult with an insurance professional for further explanation.

- <u>Long-Term Care Insurance-</u> This type of insurance pays expenses to assisted-living facilities. Assisted-living facilities (ALF) care for people who cannot live independently due to illness, and/or elderly care). This is a policy, which you may or may not utilized during your lifespan, but many people feel a 'peace-of-mind' mentality in knowing their family members will not be responsible for their care in the event a serious medical condition arises or for their elderly care. It also removes a concern for those who do not have family, and would like to know they have arranged to receive good care for themselves.

STRESS IS A BITCH!

Superheroes dealing with stress in comparison to how 'us' old farts handle stress, in many scenarios, are quite different. 'Us' old farts have been on the planet longer, therefore, we all know stress happens and problems arise. Problems create stress for people of all ages, but with age and life experiences, comes skills for resolving issues in a logical manner (at least it should).

Another reason some people deal with stressful problems better than others is one simple fact— they have money in the bank! The old cliché, "Money is Not Everything," is true (your health is everything), but money is a great tool for removing stress, which is associated with not having any damn money! When you begin working, consider micro-managing your paycheck into categories—
- Monthly bills
- *Reasonable* entertainment allowance
- 'Pay Myself First' (save money)

Disciplining yourself with responsible money management habits will result in an ever-growing savings account, which results in *saving-your-ass* from a stressful situation.

As for the stressful situations you may encounter, which have nothing to do with money issues, put forth your best efforts to resolve the situation calmly and logically— in doing so, your emotional health will benefit.

Adults should self-educate themselves about money management. There are many internet resources available—in-addition, you may want to consider having a consultation with a financial advisor/planner through your local bank or with a local financial planning/investment company.

Lessons are learned by experiencing the 'good' and the 'not-so-good' events occurring in our daily lives. All any of us (the old farts & the superheroes) can do is move onward and appreciate all of our stress-free days.

GIVE ME SOME CREDIT!

Every adult has a responsibility to learn how financial institutions view and report credit ratings, in both negative and positive ways.

There are many websites with information about establishing credit, along with resources explaining the credit reporting process—this page is your reminder to get busy and start educating yourself, your credit score will affect you throughout your life!

Many people abuse the credit lines given to them by overcharging on items they do not really need, which results in creating a new monthly bill.
Using your newly issued credit to charge items you are accustomed to paying for with cash, is a great way to build a positive credit score— set aside the cash and pay those credit card charges in full each month—this will result in obtaining and retaining a higher credit score. In addition, each year you should review your three credit reports for accuracy...you would be amazed by the mistakes people have discovered on their credit reports.

If you choose not establish credit for yourself, you may find out later down the road, when you want to finance a new vehicle or purchase your first home, a lender may not be willing to approve your application simply because they cannot view a financial repayment history—it won't be personal—it's just business!

The sooner you take the time to self-educate yourself on this topic, the sooner someone will give you some damn credit!

MIND YOUR OWN
BUSINESS!

This section is for those superheroes who would like to be an entrepreneur. If this is you and you are convinced that you have the superpowers to create a business service or a business product, then you should continue reading.

There will be much to learn and to research for your business plan in order to make your business dream a reality. The more you research and plan—the greater your chances will be for success!

The following list may be helpful in sending your ambitious superhero-ass in the right direction!

- Research the industry you will be working in and educate yourself thoroughly.
- Make a list of information based on what your competitors offer as far as products, services, prices, discounts, warranties, and who are their target customers.

- Once you evaluate your research, decide if this is a business worth investing your time and money into— you do not want to create a job for yourself, which you may not enjoy doing!
- Decide how you will fund the start-up costs and the operational costs. If you have difficulties in finding investors or obtaining a business loan, you may want to research the various 'Crowd-Funding' websites and begin a business 'start-up' project in hopes people will donate towards your dream.
- Devise a business plan and include details: employees, and/or subcontractors, business liability insurance, your marketing budget, your salary (for a year) etc. Research online and review the many resourceful websites with entrepreneurial content. Decide on a business name, and check with your state's incorporation records to ensure the business name is available for you to use. Many states today have searchable public-data available on their websites pertaining to the registered corporations, and helpful 'Need-To-Know' information for future/current business owners.

- Incorporate your business to protect yourself from personal liabilities. There are online websites that offer incorporation filing services and many attorneys provide this service. Your state may have a website, which allows people to file their own incorporation forms directly online. If your state offers online filings, read all the information thoroughly. Do not proceed to file forms without having a full understanding of incorporating your business. Consult with an attorney or tax professional.
- After you incorporate, you will need to file for an EIN# (Employer Identification Number) from the IRS (Internal Revenue Service).
- Once you have your business's incorporation papers and the EIN# you can open a business checking account with your local bank.
- Review the required business insurance for your industry and consult with an insurance agent.
  - ✓ Commercial Liability Insurance
  - ✓ Commercial Auto Insurance
  - ✓ Worker's Compensation
  - ✓ Health & Dental Insurance

- Inquire with your local/state government agencies on requirements of running a business in your county and obtaining the necessary business licenses/permits.
- Order your marketing materials: website, business cards, business logo, flyers, brochures, etc. There are many user-friendly websites available for you to design these items or you may want to consider hiring a graphic artist or marketing agency.
- If you open a business that sells products, then you will need to educate yourself on your state/local sales tax requirements and register your business with them or hire an accounting firm to handle all the business filings.
- Decide on your accounting method (educate yourself on cash & accrual accounting methods...most small businesses use cash), and which accounting software will best suit your business to track your expenses & income. Never commingle personal & business funds!
- If your business will be accepting credit cards, you will need to review and compare credit card merchant fees and setup your merchant account.

Opening a business is a huge responsibility! Being self-employed may be a great path for you and being an employee who wants to excel within a company may be great path—only you can out-weigh the '*pros and cons*' of this career choice!

Lastly, the IRS and the various government organizations within your state expect you to understand every aspect of operating a business. It is a big responsibility and not understanding the legalities of running a business may result in audits and financial penalties.

Many community colleges offer business courses and there are many websites offering business courses online. Obtaining knowledge for all aspects of your life is the key to a well-adjusted adult life...in other words, it's the best way to handle your shit!

Take charge of your responsibilities and put
forth your best efforts in making logical
decisions each day and you
will be a soaring superhero!
AND
One day— A long time from now—
You Will Be an Old Fart
Sharing the Wisdom
of
How You Handled Your Shit
Back when You were
A Bad-Ass, Smart-Ass
Superhero!

Printed in Great Britain
by Amazon